ABC

Alphabet Stories

This book
belongs to
Little Gold Ted's friend

_ _ _ _ _ _ _ _ _ _

Published by Vanessa Wiercioch
Publishing partner: Paragon Publishing, Rothersthorpe
First published 2021
© Vanessa Wiercioch 2021

Characters created by Poppy Satha
Illustrations created by Sasha Satha

ISBN 978-1-78222-862-2

Book design, layout and production management by Into Print
www.intoprint.net
+44 (0)1604 832149

An ABC story book with more sweet verses to complement the charming illustrations, created by Poppy and Sasha Satha, 16 year old twins.

A special message of thanks to my wonderful son Harry for his on-going support for Little Gold Ted.

The ASTRONAUT flies into outer space
Directing his rocket to the cosmic base
Doing a moon walk with upmost grace
Whilst collecting rocks for his database

Aa
Astronaut

The stripy BEE flies from flower to flower
Then into the hive, that looks like a tower
Making very sweet honey for you to devour
"Yummy honey on toast"..... in half an hour?

Bb
Buzzy Bee

CHRISTMAS is Ted's favourite time of the year
With Carols and Presents, bringing good cheer
Children staying awake hoping Santa is near
Leaving carrots and milk for Rudolph the reindeer

Cc

Christmas

66 This helmet is heavy" says Little Gold Ted

"It's made of Copper and flattens my head"

"With this suit I can DIVE, it's amazing" he said

"I can see the fish swimming along the seabed".

Dd
Diver

When Santa needs help he approaches an ELF
There's too many presents to wrap by himself
Elves pick and wrap, placing gifts on the shelf
So that Mrs Claus can tie the bows on herself

Ee
Elf

The FLAMINGO looks pink but really it's white
It has something to do with the glow of the light
It mostly likes standing but sometimes takes flight
Where a hundred together make a beautiful sight

Ff
Flamingo

Little Gold Ted is dressed as a GHOST
Pretending to frighten is what he likes most
"Woooo - hoooo" he squeals in a delighted boast
"Yooo - hooo" calls Reg, "I have marshmallows to toast!"

Gg
Ghost

Gold Ted likes to play with his HULA HOOP
He enjoys it most when he's with his group
Can he manage ten turns , in a single loop?
"I've done it" Ted says and let's out a whoop

20

Hh
Hula Hoop

An IGLOO is a home that's made from ice
Chiselled into blocks, the work is precise
Inside there's a fire, making it toasty and nice
For some it's their home, their icy paradise

I i
Igloo

In times of old, the JESTER was the court clown
Happily playing his tricks and he never would frown
Entertaining the King by wearing his Crown
Or purposely slipping and falling right down

Jj
Jester

AKING is so regal with his magnificent gown
He prefers Royal colours, which he wears into town
Always looking resplendent, from the top down
He likes it best when there's a matching crown

Kk

King

A LUMBERJACK chops up wood all day
Safety goggles on, in case chips fly astray
Hard hat, big axe, it's quite a display
Reg watches on, ensuring Ted is okay

Ll
Lumberjack

During full MOON the night-sky becomes bright
And Little Gold Ted holds his lamp very tight
It can cast strange shadows that give Ted a fright
Or show a star shooting by at the speed of light

Mm
Moon

Put on you pyjamas and jump into bed
Snuggle down comfy and read with Ted
It's time to NAP, so rest your head
There are sweet dreams that lie ahead

Nn
Nap Time

Gold Ted stands on the stage, conducting the band
Controlling the tempo with the wave of his hand
Whilst tapping his baton on the music stand
Where the sound of the ORCHESTRA is very grand

Oo
Orchestra

PENGUINS can live in climates, where it snows a lot
Meaning it's ever so cold and just doesn't get hot
But if you visit the zoo they have a special spot
Where they swim in the pool, or do their wobbly trot

Pp
Penguin

Before there were pens, we wrote with a QUILL
Ted tried it today and said "it's quite a skill"
You must focus hard and keep very still
Just don't knock the pot or the ink will spill

Qq
Quill

REG the Rat, is Ted's mentor and friend
He's wise and kind; on him Ted can depend
Cheering Ted on, for whatever's on trend
Having fun together, almost every weekend

Rr
Reg

Little Gold Ted loves a good soak in the bath
Full of bubbles and SOAP, he has quite a laugh
'Splish-sploshing' around, he makes a watery path
Think it's time to mop up this soggy aftermath

Ss
Soap Bath

The TELEPHONE BOX is where everything's said
It brightens the street with its colour of red
People queue up outside, including Gold Ted
With his purse full of coins, he keeps the phone fed

Tt
Telephone Box

An UMBRELLA keeps you dry when it's pouring with rain

But when it gets windy, it can be quite a pain

As holding it upright is somewhat a strain

And sometimes you take-off, much like a plane

Uu
Umbrella

He may look like a doctor but he's actually a VET
And the job he does, is to look after your pet
The vets kind and friendly and says "please don't fret"
"He's a beautiful Puppy who deserves a rosette"

Vv
Vet

Little Gold Ted loves his WELLINGTON boots
Splashing through puddles and causing disputes
The cars passing by giving cheery 'TOOT TOOTS'
Ted has so much fun on his muddy commutes

Ww
Wellington

To see in your body you need an X-RAY
Your insides look strange and a little bit grey
"When I count to three, very still you must stay
Then off you go home, to have a good play"

Xx
X-ray

Ted chooses YOGA for his exercise
How high do you think his leg can rise?
"Oh this is so hard" Ted gently sighs
"Be serious Ted", does the teacher chastise

Y y
Yoga

A ZOO-KEEPER'S job has many odd parts
Feeding and bedtime is written on charts

A quick morning cuddle, then playtime starts

But most of all, it's about sharing our hearts

Zz
Zoo Keeper

Lightning Source UK Ltd.
Milton Keynes UK
UKHW050327130422
401464UK00005B/96